The Prices We Pay

stories by

Rayshell Clapper

Finishing Line Press
Georgetown, Kentucky

The Prices We Pay

ACKNOWLEDGMENTS

There are so very many people to thank. A body of work does not come from a solitary place. Let me start, though, with my writing mentors, Rilla Askew, Kat Meads, and Lou Berney. Their keen eyes and dedication to helping me grow as a writer inspired me. I could not have written these stories without their encouragement and guidance.

Many thanks also to go to Jayne Shimko, Melanie Brake, and Moose Tyler. Each of you workshopped these pieces and helped me shape them from their first messy drafts into stories I cherish. I'm blessed by your talent. I'm blessed by your friendship. Thank you.

And I'm blessed with the best of friends. To my besties, Bri Duke and Jessica Isaacs, who encouraged and supported me with love and enthusiasm. I'm a better person and a better writer because of you. Thanks also go to out to my dearest friends who put up with me during this process: Chalisse Forgette, Lisa Ang, Megan Hansen, Dorian Eidhin, Alan Haslam, Ky George, and Jason Carrick. You each helped me see that it's okay to be excited. Your love and support are precious to me. I'm so thankful the universe brought us together.

Thanks also to my family for a lifetime of lessons. I love you.

Finally, thanks go out to my partner, my love, Christian Morgan. I know I'm fussy. I know I'm especially fussy when writing. But you love and encourage me the entire time. Thank you.

Publisher: Leah Huete de Maines
Editor: Christen Kincaid
Cover Art: Laura Kaiser
Author Photo: Carley Porter
Cover Design: Elizabeth Maines McCleavy

Order online: www.finishinglinepress.com
also available on amazon.com

Author inquiries and mail orders:
Finishing Line Press
PO Box 1626
Georgetown, Kentucky 40324
USA

Table of Contents

Table of Contents

For my mom who wanted me to write happy stories.
These may not be exactly happy endings, but the truth and love of
them come from the truth and love she has shown me my entire life.

And for my nieces and nephews.
May you always remember that love is worth the prices we pay.

And may you always know that you are loved.

For Daddy. Always.

Bat Versus Mosquito

Mosquito flapped its wings slow after her recent feast. The human hadn't even noticed her gulping away at his blood. Mosquito giggled to herself, forcing a burp full of blood to burst from her sucker. She wiped it against her wing and giggled again. Mosquito was loopy from her feast, fat and happy and drunk. Instead of the high-pitched whir of her wings, she made almost no noise, moving lazy and slow. Her wings stuttered; she felt the sleepy pull of a nap. Landing with a soft bump, she curled up at the base of a large oak tree's trunk. Mosquito knew she shouldn't have engorged herself on dinner. There would be more to feast on tomorrow, but the taste had been so sweet, so thick and enriching, and it'd been so long since she'd enjoyed such a treat. Her eyes heavy, belly full, she whispered just before sleep took her, "I really should move to a safer spot. Too open," as her eyelids shut.

Mosquito snored in her stupor as Bat perched high in the tree canopies. Minutes before, Bat had called and called, had waited for the right sound to bounce back to her. And then she smiled; her lungs caught with the echo. It wasn't Mosquito's giggles or burps that sent back what Bat was waiting to hear; it was the slow flap of the bug's wings, so lacking their usual frenetic buzz. Mosquito's crash landing just below Bat: fortuitous. Bat smiled and swooped on the silent breeze to Mosquito, settling in front of her, still unnoticed by the little pest. Bat's smile widened. She, too, would have her feast.

Rabbit Saves Snake

Snake coiled up tighter, trying to make his cold blood warm within his body. It wasn't working. The day had begun comfortable: sunny and warm. Snake drew on its rays and slithered all over and up the mountain in search of breakfast. But Snake had climbed too high, had been too confident, and the cold air did as it does to his cold blood. His scales shivered in his coil. His eyes kissed together, and then he jerked them open and tried, again, to move.

The only sound about him was the wind. He flicked his tongue but sensed only flora. He had to do something to save himself. With every drop of circulating blood, he lifted his head and tail. He began to shake that tail, the purr of the rattle echoed around him, and he collapsed.

Here, here is where I die, he thought, *on this forsaken mountain.* His foolishness would end in forever closing his eyes. He glanced to the trail to see beams of sunlight. If only he could get to those, maybe, just maybe he'd warm inch-by-inch and be able to slink one vertebrae at a time down the mountain path. Alas, though, he couldn't even shiver his scales anymore. All was lost.

And then he heard it—the hippity-hoppity of long legs, the rustle of brush, and the humming of a rabbit. The warm-blooded beast—Snake's most favorite prey—hopped right up to the reptile, oblivious. *Rabbit?!*, Snake thought to himself. *Not the brightest mammal.* And an idea formed in Snake's head.

"Help, pleasssse," Snake pled, his voice not even a whisper. This stopped Rabbit cold. It didn't move. Snake flicked its tongue again and tasted the testosterone swirling around it. Male, young and scared. *Things are looking up*, Snake thought.

"Wh…what're you doing there?" Rabbit asked as he stepped back from Snake's reach. "I…I…I'll leave you to it." He turned to hop back down the mountainside but was stopped by Snake's last, pathetic try to rattle his tail.

"Pleasssse, pleasssse help me. I need to get down the mountain or else I die." Snake's voice slurred a bit as more of his blood froze. He had trouble keeping his eyes open.

"I don't know…don't know." Rabbit stepped closer. "You'll eat me once your blood warms."

"No, I promisssse. I jusssst want to go home, back to my hole. I promissssse." Each word slithered out Snake's mouth, slow and sibilant.

Rabbit hopped around Snake, looking for tricks. He hopped to the trail and looked at how far down the mountain he'd have to drag Snake. Then he hopped back over.

Rabbit squinted his eyes and pointed at Snake. "You promise? 'Cause this won't be easy."

Snake nodded. "I promisssse."

"Pinky promise?" Rabbit stuck out his paw. He laughed at himself. "Ooops. Sorry. Okay, let's go."

Rabbit lifted Snake—coiled and stiff—over his head, wrapping the reptile around his neck and shoulders. He noticed how cold the snake was. Rabbit just shrugged. Down the mountain they went. Hop-by-hop, Snake could feel the air warming, the sun's rays beaming onto his scales, his blood pumping thinner, faster throughout his body. He could almost move now. And before he knew it, Rabbit had hopped right down to the base of the mountain, stopping right in the sunniest spot on the path.

Rabbit was having so much fun hopping down the mountain, enjoying the sights, that he didn't even notice Snake writhing on his shoulders ever-so-slowly. He stopped to flare his little nostrils in the wind, feel it playing with his fur. Rabbit smiled; helping Snake was good.

3

He bowed to the ground so Snake could slip off his shoulders. Then Rabbit hopped up and faced his new friend, bouncing from foot to foot. Snake coiled up again, this time his head held high and his rattle pricked up.

"I want to thank you, Rabbit, for your kindness," Snake began. He closed his eyes and shook his head a bit. He could feel the tingle that Rabbit's scent stirred in him. "Now, though, you must run." Snake's mouth stood agape, fangs glinting in the sun, but his eyes drooped. If he could cry, he would have then.

Rabbit cocked his head left, then right. He shivered. Snake flicked his tongue, his eyes narrowing. He tasted the testosterone again. Rabbit hopped a step back.

"But...you promised?" Rabbit's accusation came out a whisper as he held Snake's gaze. Rabbit's shoulders squared.

"I can't help it. I am a snake," Snake shivered his scales, the rattle loud again. "And you are my prey. You knew what I was when you picked me up. But I wanted to give you at least a chance." Snake started to weave, right to left, Rabbit's chin quivering as he watched hypnotized by the murmur of the rattle, warning and lulling. Rabbit slumped. Snake undulated with an internal countdown.

Rabbit shook himself out of the trance and squinted at Snake. And then he did what Snake didn't expect; he jumped over Snake's head, leaping high into the air and landing behind his predator. Instinct kicking in, Snake struck at him as he soared over the reptile, scraping his underbelly with a poisoned fang. Snake uncoiled then and slithered around to find Rabbit had hippity-hopped back up the mountain a few feet. He stopped, waving down at Snake.

"You knew what I was when I picked you up," Rabbit called down. Snake flicked his tongue and smiled. Rabbit's adrenaline smelled good.

"Until next time…" Rabbit stopped, his eyes widening as his mouth watered and his body flopped to the ground. Snake slithered over then, looking down at his savior. Pain writhed through Rabbit, legs jerking, eyes wide. His mouth spewed froth. And Snake did the grateful thing. He struck at Rabbit's heart, spreading his venom faster. Rabbit laid stiff, so Snake opened his mouth gaping wide, and began the task of feeding.

How Vulture Lost Her Plume

Vulture glided on the rippling currents of the wind, the wind carrying her wherever it wanted. She had no place to be, no one to see. All she had was the faraway sun's rays to warm her and hundreds of feet of air between her and the ground. She moved slow, steady, only inches at a time toward nowhere. Toward anywhere. But it felt good, the wind's hug holding her steady. She opened her beak to taste the current—fresh, earthy, clean.

Vulture soared high in the sky, circling slow and calm above the creek. Her wings spread so that the breeze could catch her, hold her up, and take her spinning wide and slow to the earth. As she circled down, she saw a family of foxes—a mother, father, and two kits—playing in the creek, splish-splashing in the water, chasing each other. Vulture sighed as she made her way to the nearest tree branch. She outstretched her talons, spreading each one so that she could grasp the branch. Her talons only wrapped about halfway around the wood, the bark tickling underneath her as she gripped and settled her body down, ruffling and resting her feathers. She looked down at the canines, tussling and laughing. She saw the young kits bouncing from mother to creek and back again. Oh, their energy, thought Vulture. Then she closed her eyes and listened.

No sooner had she done this than she heard the smallest fox shout, "Hey, Vulture, get outta here. No one wants to share your lunch."

Vulture fluttered her eyes open and looked down at him. She saw only a cocky smirk and his tongue hanging out the side of his mouth. Then he flopped down to the ground with a thump. Vulture watched him, eyes scrunched to see better.

The small fox rolled onto his side, first right, then left, and then again and again, and he laughed. His sister fox rolled and laughed with him. The cacophony echoed throughout Vulture's mind into her heart. Their cackle crackled with the leaves underneath them. But not for long. Mother Fox marched over to him, grabbed him by the nape of his neck, and pulled him upright. Mother Fox let go and backed up, staring into his eyes. She flared her nostrils at him. Then, she cut her eyes at Sister Fox, who skittered behind the Sycamore, tail tucked and quivering. Vulture saw Mother Fox's every movement as she stalked toward them and couldn't imagine how the kits felt but knew it couldn't be good. The small fox stopped laughing; clearly, Mother Fox meant business. Vulture smiled down at them.

"Oh no, Son Child. Don't you poke fun at Vulture. You have no idea her sacrifice for us."

Son Child whined, high and long, before saying, "But, Momma, she's so ugly, look at her. And she eats dead things. Bleck!" He shook his head, his tongue swinging, hitting his cheeks. Son Child used his snout to point up at Vulture, who sat, hulked on the branch, the sun's beams haloing around her, her shadow thrown onto the foxes below. She didn't move. "I mean, that head without feathers?"

Mother Fox shook her head. "She can't help her Nature any more than you can help yours. Remember that time you chased your tail for hours because you couldn't catch it? Felt silly, didn't you? Well, that's Nature." Son Child ducked his head and huffed into the dirt. Vulture scoffed, imagining the little fox twirling and twirling trying to figure out what his tail was. Mother Fox continued, "Vulture wasn't always bald. In fact, she wears that baldness as a badge, a reminder to us all of her sacrifice."

Son Child cocked his head first right, then left, panting. He looked to Vulture, who looked right back at him, then he turned back to his mother. Vulture watched a second longer, then squinted her eyes. *I don't want to miss this*, she thought. She kept her ears trained on the story below. Once again, she opened her beak to let the wind cool her down.

"Sit down, Son Child. Sister Girl, come here. Let me tell you the story of how Vulture lost her plume." The smallest fox circled and then settled on his haunches in front of his mother, who sat back on her own haunches as Sister Girl settled next to her brother.

"Once, very long ago, Vulture had a most awesome plume on her head, tall and full of feathers silky black and waving in the wind. She wore her feathers with grace as these defined Vulture from her fellow birds. In fact, despite her size, amongst the largest of the bird world, Vulture was a model of grace and love, welcoming all around her. And other beasts loved her, for she did not hunt them like Eagle, Owl, or Hawk. She patiently waited for Nature to take its course, then played her role in the circle of life on the carcasses left over. She found sustenance in what none wanted. See, Son Child, Vulture lives without having to kill. She is the eternal giver of our world. But it is not in this action that we know this most. It is in how she saved us all."

"Many years ago, in the beginning of time, Sun wanted to be closer to us. He'd watched and watched and fell in love with us all. He wanted to say hello, to play with us, to be near." Mother Fox glanced at Vulture, who opened her eyes and looked up to mighty Sun distant in the sky, in space, but still near, ever near. She nodded her head at him, her gaze then dropping to Mother Fox. The wind rushed into her mouth, soothing her.

"That sounds fun," Son Child said, his tail twitching under him. His paws began to quiver. Even Sister Girl's ears perked. Vulture could tell they were all in now.

"Yes, it does sound fun, but Sun is very, very hot, hotter than anything we've ever felt." She bent low then, looking her kit in the eyes again. Vulture hunched a bit more. "You remember that time lightning struck our den?"

Son Child's eyes widened; his ears perked taller. He stood and then sat back on his haunches, a small whimper slipping out. His mother pulled herself back up to sit upright. Vulture shivered a bit, her feathers waving and then resettling. She knew well what worried Son Child.

They'd had to rebuild so much of their home after the lightening strike. And they were lucky.

"Good. Then you understand a bit of the Sun's power. Yes, indeed, playing sounds fun, but Sun's fingers left only crispy critters. Time and again, Sun tried to come play only to leave carcass after carcass singed to just ash and bone. Sun left bodies in his wake; they were nearly just powder. One touch and they would float away on the wind, dust to dust, ash to ash. We watched as family and friends blew away in the breeze. We wept. We raged. Then we ran. The animals of Earth went into hiding. We didn't know what else to do. Day after day, we hid from Sun's attempts to make contact. And we started to wither away. If Sun didn't kill us, thirst and hunger would. We grew desperate."

At this, Vulture closed her eyes again. She remembered this as all Vultures do. The story is passed from mother to daughter, father to son, parent to child, generation to generation. And with it, the pain of the memory of the animals of Earth. She opened her eyes again to look down, her gaze locking with Mother Fox's. Vulture's eyes watered. She untucked her wings, tucked them again, and then let out a quiet hiss, long and slow. Vulture watched as one tear snuck down Mother Fox's face, plopping on her paw. Vulture blinked away her own.

"What happened, Momma?" The little kits now stood on all fours, tails tucked, all in for the story.

"Well, Son Child, Sister Girl, one night, Vulture floated high above the tree tops, thinking and thinking about how to fix this. Talking to Sun hadn't worked. But maybe Vulture could do something else. Her plume was large and tough, her wings beautiful and mighty, her body thick and strong. She flew higher and higher, all night long, toward the east where Sun woke up."

Sister Girl sat back on her hind legs, but she was all ears, focused on Mother Fox's words. Son Child hopped from paw to paw now, so engaged in the story. He'd not looked up at Vulture since Mother Fox began, forgetting all about what had started this story: Vulture above him, watching from the branch. But Vulture hadn't forgotten them. She listened now, neck bowed and head twisted to hear every word, every movement the foxes made. She could smell the kits and their excitement, all musky and earthy. She smiled, bringing her beak back together.

Mother Fox continued, "Yes, higher and higher she went until the Sun reached out for its morning stretch. It was then that Vulture flapped her wings, all six feet of them, to catch the wind. She tucked her head just as her giant plume collided with Sun. Vulture flapped and flapped, pushing harder and harder, Sun moving inches at first, then feet. With that, Vulture flapped once, twice, thrice more and pounded her plumed head into Sun until all her might and power sent Sun spinning through space, back to his own home. Vulture fell back then, plummeting to terra firma. But wind caught her in its arms, settling her down circle by circle until she rested on the ground."

"But Momma, the fire, the Sun's fire," Son Child said. He whimpered then, the sound coming from deep in his heart, his own mouth frowning. Mother Fox nodded her head, closed her eyes, and continued.

"Yes. Sun's fire had done its damage. Though Vulture was strong and her plume mighty, Sun's power took its toll. Sun never came back to play with us again, yet Vulture was left with no plume and only a wrinkled, bald head for all to see." She dropped her own head for a second, then looked back up to Vulture. "For all to remember."

Son Child followed his mother's gaze. Sister Girl nipped at his ear. He made eye contact with Vulture but quickly ducked his head and looked down at his paws. Mother Fox walked up to him, nudged his shoulders with her snout, then nodded toward Vulture. Son Child took one, two, three steps toward the massive bird settled above him.

"Um, Vulture?" Son Child sat back on his haunches and looked up again, eyes glistening. Vulture cocked her head, eyes fixed on Son Child. "I, uh, I'm real sorry for laughing at you and calling you ugly and everything. I mean, I didn't know about, uh, all that you did."

Vulture looked over at Mother Fox, who nodded. Then she spread her wings, feeling for the wind, and flapped to glide down to Son Child. The wind fingered through his fur, his coat, his ears, his tail, hugging him as she landed next to him, just as the wind hugged her when in flight. She swept her wing around him, enwrapping him completely. Then she looked to Sister Girl and opened her other wing. The little fox trotted over and snuggled in. Mother Fox looked on and smiled.

And Vulture said, "It is my honor. And someday, if you ever have to protect the forest, the earth, the flora and the fauna, so it will be your honor. We all play our part, little ones. You and me. We all play our part."

Coyote Meets Herself

This is how it all started for Little Coyote. Little Coyote peeped her head out the opening of her den, wandering from her little cave under the big rock. She looked left, then right. Then she stepped one paw out, followed by the other, step-by-step until her whole body was out in the forest. She looked left, then right again. And then a third time.

"Momma," she whispered. Birds fluttered from a bush, and Little Coyote scampered back into the den. She huddled down and looked out at the brush and trees, the flowers and bushes.

"Papa," she called a little louder, her voice ricocheting off the walls of her family's home, rebounding out the den opening and up into the world.

Still nothing.

Once again, she poked out of her den. She put her nose to the ground, sniffed, hoping for Momma's and Papa's scents. Nothing. She went back, circled once, twice, thrice, and curled her body up, facing the entrance so that she could see everything. And she waited, her stomach growling and gurgling underneath her.

One day, not that long ago but too long for comfort, Little Coyote's parents had left to hunt for food. She'd waited and waited and waited for them. Days and more days had passed with no sign of Momma Coyote and Papa Coyote, and Little Coyote had run out of food and water. She'd grown so very hungry and so very lonely. And she was so very scared. She knew that something awful must have happened for her parents to not return. The worst kind of awful. Longing trickled down her face, falling to the ground beneath her. She let out a long yowl in their honor. It echoed throughout the den.

She was all alone now. She howled again. *What a cruel world*, thought Little Coyote. She padded back and forth in her den. Her stomach roared at her this time. Yesterday morning she'd eaten the last of her stores. Her mind swirled. She needed food and water. Her mouth salivated at these thoughts, and she panted ever more.

Finally, she stopped in front of the entrance and sat back on her hind legs, looking out into the great wide open. Full pine and lanky aspen towered over her, looking down on but also protecting. Sagebrush and juniper peppered the forest floor with a smattering of columbines and clover. She raised her snout and sniffed the air, taking in the scents of the familiar plants and trees. This was her home, all she'd ever known. But now, she would have to find something more. She would have to venture beyond her little forest cove. The world was so large, and she was so small. But she was also so hungry.

"If I'm going to live," she said aloud, "then I have to find my way."

She raised up and turned to the only home she'd known. She would miss its safety. She would miss the smell of her momma and papa. She would miss how cool it was and the darkness that enveloped her in comfort. The sun could be so unforgiving outside, after all. But she had to figure out how to live.

"I'll be back," she promised. So she trotted out of the den. She made it only a few steps before turning back. She went and looked in. It was a good den, and she would want it back some day, so she lifted her hind leg—just like Papa did oh-so-many times—and marked the entrance. Then she pulled some leaves and branches in front and marked them too, this time squatting, much more her style. She nodded to herself, satisfied. She turned and took her first steps into the big wide world.

"Here, I will find a new band," she said to the trees in the forest. "But first, food and water."

Little Coyote didn't know how to hunt, but she did know that the forest was abundant with fruits and grasses. These would suffice for now. So she weaved through the trees, in and out and all around, looking for food and predators. The woodlands could hide so many threats.

"Little Coyote, watch out for the hairless, two-legged beasts who walk upright. They're called humans. And they can't be trusted." Her momma's words echoed in her mind.

Momma Coyote had taught her that, at least. And though she'd never seen these humans, she knew that anything on two legs was a threat. So she stepped one paw in front of the other, glancing this way and that, moving slow and steady for food . . . and to find acceptance.

She raised her snout to sniff the air, seeking any scent of fruit or water or anything unfamiliar, dangerous. Her nostrils flared and flared again as the breeze filled them. She closed her eyes and let the wind ruffle through her coat. It hummed in her ears telling her sweet nothings, not the least of which was where to find water. She turned to her right and trotted down the path toward the trickle of water. And then she saw a creek large enough for her to lap water and cool her paws. Beside the creek, a berry bush hung heavy with delicious, plump, red berries.

"This'll do," she said, and she started munching the berries one by one. Step one of her journey completed, she sought out a bush under which she could rest protected from anything unfamiliar. She'd had a big day, after all, and she was just a little pup.

Little Coyote woke up to the sounds of chirping and scuttling and flapping and splashing. She opened her eyes and saw a flock of feathered beasts playing in the creek. She'd seen them before, flying through the aspen and pines and cottonwoods in her woodlands. She remembered her papa calling them something, something that sounded silly to Little Coyote. She closed her eyes.

"Oh right," she whispered to herself. "Titmouse, Papa had named them titmouse, and they were birds."

She watched for a while as the birds clearly loved being together. She knew they must be a band. And all Little Coyote wanted was to be a part of a band again. So she crept out from the bush, her stomach low to the ground. She didn't want to scare the little birds. Inch-by-inch, she crawled closer to them. They didn't seem to mind. They just kept chittering and fluttering their wings, hopping from branch to branch. If it were her, she would have smelled something coming closer, and if she didn't attack or run, then that meant she accepted it. *They must want me!* Her heart thumped with the thought. Poor Little Coyote knew so little about the world.

Little Coyote smiled. She just might have found acceptance. Alas, though, Little Coyote cracked a branch, and the birds turned, saw her, and immediately took flight up to the tree tops. They chirped and squawked at her from above.

"Go away," said a small one.

"We don't want you here," said another one.

"You can't eat us," said a third, the largest, their leader. It stood feathers plumped, chest thrust.

Little Coyote cocked her head and furrowed her brow.

"I don't want to eat you," she yelped up to them. "I just want to find where I belong. Is it with you?"

The birds looked from one to another and then back down to the carnivore at the base of the tree. They'd never had a coyote as a sister, mother, grandmother, or friend. Heck, they'd never had a coyote as anything other than danger. They burst into laughter, rocking the branches back and forth with their mirth.

"You silly. Coyotes eat birds. We're not falling for your trick," said that same largest bird. And with a quick whoosh, the birds left the tree and Little Coyote empty.

She flopped down on her side and lay there all alone. Another yowl left her throat. Tiny droplets again slid down her face into the dirt underneath her. She sighed, picked herself up, and started upstream. *Where there's water, there will be other animals.* It was her only hope at finding a place to belong.

Not long after, Little Coyote came up to a family of foxes—Mother Fox with two kits. Little Coyote stopped and hid behind a large oak tree. She peeked around the side and watched. Again, she didn't want to scare the fox family, but she did want to see if this might be where she belonged. They so looked like a family that would accept her. Heck, she even kinda looked like them.

Mother Fox lay curled up near the two kits. She watched as the two little ones rolled around and wrestled each other.

"Grr...I've got you pinned," said the smaller, more golden-colored fox as he had the other's ear in his jaws. "Give in."

The larger kit stopped moving for a second. Little Coyote smiled as she watched this one contemplate the next move. If Little Coyote had been pinned, she would have nipped at the fox's neck and flipped on top. That'd win the game. Instead, the bigger fox whimpered. Little Coyote watched as Mother Fox raised her head and looked over at her tousling kits. Seeing nothing worrisome, she laid her head back on her paws and closed her eyes. Little Coyote's heart hiccupped then, thinking of her own mother.

The bigger fox whimpered again.

"Say the word." With his mouth full of her ear, the words came out a bit jumbled, but the little fox was determined.

And though Little Coyote couldn't know, the little fox was biting hard. He'd pierced through his sister's ear with his razor-sharp, pinprick teeth. He pulled at her ear a bit harder to get her to give in, but she only whimpered louder. What Little Coyote didn't know was that's how foxes play. She'd never played with another pup of any species. She didn't know much about this kind of fun. But she didn't like that the pinned kit was in pain. So, she stepped out from her hiding spot and shot forward toward the two playing to help the fallen fox. In Little Coyote's mind, she would tag in, and they'd win. Before she could get anywhere close, though, Mother Fox sprang to action and swooped in front of her kits, baring teeth, ready to kill.

That stopped Little Coyote hard, so hard she tumbled over her paws and landed sprawled out in front of Mother Fox.

"I think not, sneaky coyote." Her snarl followed, her fur standing all along her back, and Little Coyote shivered. With eyes wide and wet, Little Coyote stared at this protector. And though she should have been afraid, all she could think about was her own mother and how she would have given her life to save her pup. She did give her life, for all Little Coyote knew. Again, a yowl slipped out, and she couldn't help it, so she ran to Mother Fox and snuggled up to her chest, wailing into her coat. Mother Fox stood stiff, still, and silent. Little Coyote's grief wet on her chest, she pushed her away and shook her head. She bared her teeth again in warning.

"What are you doing, coyote? I'm not your mother. Go. Shoo." She snapped, jaws clanking, and swiped her paw in front of her. Little Coyote watched the paw.

"But," she began.

"No." Mother Fox bared her teeth again.

Little Coyote's head bowed low, snout dragging the ground just enough to leave a path, she sniffled and started back upriver. She missed her mom and dad. She missed her den. She missed that old life. Images of the birds bathing and the foxes wrestling floated through her mind. Her heart ached more.

She paid only the slightest attention to where she was going. Her only guide was the bubbling and swishing of the creek next to her. And before she knew it, she'd stepped out of the woodlands and into something new. She froze. There, in front of her, was human life. She watched the humans working throughout, standing on just two legs, scratching at the ground, cleaning the outside, playing in the creek. They moved about talking to each other and exchanging goods. She heard the rattling of something passing on the dirt path that cut the village in half. Glancing around, her chest started to pound. She'd not met humans before, and she didn't know much more about them than to avoid them. The pounding inside her turned to a shiver. She looked at the homes in front of her and cocked her head. Where were the holes in the ground, the dens, the trees? What about the bushes and woodland animals? Why was everything so open and yet also so closed off? Little Coyote whimpered quietly.

She backed away one step at a time into the safety of the forest. This new weirdness frightened her, so she found a bush in which to hide. She crawled into the middle and circled once, twice, three times, and then settled into a ball, her head resting on her front paws. It was just a little too much for her. She would rest until the moon came up to light her way.

And then, she thought to herself as sleep inched its way over her. *Then, I'll find my new family.*

Little Coyote woke later to the sounds of human cubs laughing and yelling and playing not far from her little hiding spot. The sun was dropping to his sleep, and rays of light dotted here and there. She watched the humans run around and around and then all fall to the ground, singing and giggling the entire time. She sighed. Oh, how she wanted to experience such play. But her mother's warnings shouted at her to stay away from this band. Humans were not going to be her new family.

Then she heard a new sound. A bark! And just beyond the playing group of little humans she saw a group of puppies—dog, not coyote, but still—playing and wrestling and nipping at each other's heels. The group was on the outskirts of the little humans, making their way toward her.

"This is it!" thought Little Coyote. Of course, her new family would definitely be dogs. She was, after all, herself a cousin, so naturally they'd accept her. Her little tail wagged and wagged as she watched the puppies play, inching closer and closer to her. She put her little rump into the air, ready to pounce and add to their fun. Her tongue even lolled out, so happy she was.

And then the air changed, and the puppies stopped and turned toward the new smell. They scrunched their eyes and stepped carefully, one paw at a time toward her, low growls rumbling through their group. Protection replaced their playfulness. But Little Coyote didn't know the difference. She just thought this was another game. And so she popped out at them, tail wagging, hopping from paw to paw, running through them, and nipping at their heels.

And the puppies just howled. Little Coyote stopped and cocked her head.

"Why are you scared? We're just playing," she asked the group.

"Momma told us not to play with wild dogs. She says you're uncivilized and don't even live in a house," the largest puppy answered. He was clearly the Alpha in this pack, standing tall and strong. He, like the others, was a black dog, from tips of the ears to tail. Little Coyote looked a pittance next to him with her light dusty fur, fluffy tail, and shorter legs. The Alpha's words had stung.

"Well, I don't know much, but I do know that I'm civilized. At least as civilized as you." Tears welled up but didn't drop. She would control them this time.

"Not if you don't have a house," Alpha said and turned to lead the pack back.

"Wait," Little Coyote followed. "Please can't we play? I so want a family, and yours looks happy."

The cackle of the puppies' collective laughs stung even more. They wouldn't even consider letting her join in their fun. Little Coyote dropped her head and sniffled.

"Go back to the woods, Wild Dog. You don't belong here with us civilized and beloved dogs." Alpha's words followed Little Coyote, taunting her as she walked through the woods beside the village.
Sounds of laughter and happiness filled her ears. She could smell roasting meats and fresh fruits and veggies and hear the clank of food hitting bowls. Her stomach growled.

"I'd give all the food in the world just to be accepted into a family." She sobbed as she padded near the village.

And that's when she found the cat, a large black and white village cat all sprawled out on a branch above her head. It yawned and snapped its teeth together, getting Little Coyote's attention; her eyes widened. She'd not seen such a cat before and so close to the humans. It was brave.

"You're almost as big as me," she said to it as she sat back on her haunches to get a closer look.

The black and white swished its tail. "And proud of it. No dog will mess with me." The voice purred, melodic and feminine. This feline was a girl like Little Coyote. She looked closer at the beast below her then. "You're not a dog?"

She shook her head. "Nope. They're mean. I'm just a cousin to them. I'm a coyote."

"Coyote, eh? I guess that's okay. I've known a couple of you. Good animals."

"There are other coyotes near?" Her tail began twitching under her, and she fidgeted her weight from one paw to another. The cat smiled.

"Oh, sure. They come along sometimes, wandering through the village and rummaging through trash." She paused. "Come to think of it, they always come alone. Like you. I've never seen a group together." The little cat furrowed her brow and plumped her mouth in deep contemplation. "Nope. Never in pairs or groups. Always just by themselves."

Little Coyote cocked her head to the left. She couldn't quite get all the cat's chatter.

"You're new here." It wasn't a question. Little Coyote nodded.

And Little Coyote told her story to this big cat lounging above her. She told of the birds who flew away (to which the cat licked her lips). She told of the fox and the humans and the puppies (she hissed at all). The cat listened to the coyote's search for acceptance. And then she just shook her head.

"Pup, you've got it all wrong. You don't need a family. You don't need anything else. See, you're a coyote. So what if the birds or foxes or puppies or even I don't want you? You don't need them. You're strongest alone. That's why I never see more than one coyote pawing the village

trash or stalking through the woodlands. Coyotes don't live in packs."
Again, her bushy tail swished behind her. She turned to look at it, eyes
wide and a little suspicious, Little Coyote saw. She understood that.
Her own tail often surprised her.

"Strongest alone," she said back, whispering more to herself than to the
cat. "But how do I do that?"

The cat yawned again and just stared at the coyote who clearly wasn't
going anywhere. She stood and arched her back to stretch and then
jumped down, landing on her four paws without a sound. She stood in
front of Little Coyote now, glowing green cat eyes slitted to stare into
her own round ochre coyote eyes.

"Do like me. I'm stronger alone, too, and I just do what I want. I eat
what I want and when. I lounge where I want," and at this she nodded
her head back to the branch for evidence. "I go on walkabouts and
huntings and just general fun whenever I want." She puffed a bit with
pride then. "And I don't let anyone own me. That's the thing about all
those other creatures. They are owned by others or by the collective."
And with that bit of wisdom, she stretched again and then hopped
back up to her branch to plop down, paws hanging around the branch.

Little Coyote thought back to the birds. They moved together, played
together, flew together. None had their own thoughts. Then she saw
how the foxes were owned by their mother. They couldn't take care
of themselves, not at all. She did feel a brief pang of longing for her
own mother, but also she felt proud. And finally she understood
what the dogs meant by house. The dogs had houses because humans
owned them. Plus, the Alpha spoke for the entire pack. Dogs had no
independence at all. They couldn't. Either they were owned by humans
or by the pack leader.

Little Coyote didn't have any of that. She had a den that was all hers
now. She'd proven that she could find food and water all by herself.

She'd protected herself all day by hiding and resting and sneaking about. And she'd done it all alone, just like the cat said. Little Coyote turned back toward her den, head held high, ears perked, and tail flicking as she trotted back to her home to start her new life.

Song of the Phoenix

It all started with a cough. Phoenix knew then that something just wasn't right. *When was the last time I coughed*, she wondered. She cocked her head right and left as she thought and thought and thought. She couldn't remember ever coughing.

Every morning as the Sun caressed her with its first rays, she would stretch her ruby and gold wings, feel the wind tickle through her bones, open her beak, and sing her wake-up call for Paradise. With her soft melody, the trees would shake their leaves of the night's dew, the squirrels would skitter out of their homes rushing about the forest floor, and the owls would tuck into their nooks to rest until the Moon woke them. Phoenix's song would fill them all with peace. And they'd know that the day had begun.

But this morning, when she opened up to wake the world, she coughed, a dry, quiet cough, one that came deep from within her lungs. She snapped her beak shut and brought her wings down. She flicked her eyes left and right. Alas, the world around her still slept. And of course they did. She hadn't woken them. She shifted in her nest, shimmying her tail and resettling. Then once again, she stretched her wings. She let the Sun warm them for a minute, turning her face to its rays. She felt them shroud her, energy coursing through her hollow bones. Phoenix closed her eyes and let them radiate throughout her body. She could feel the warmth coat her feathers, her body, her talons. So she opened up and tried to sing again.

Cough.

Her eyes shot open. A fire-cold shiver began deep in her heart, battling the rays of the sun. She felt her magical tear bubbling, but that tear would not save her this time. No amount of healing would save any of them.

The silence about her closed in. She remembered then what was to happen. She remembered her last cough. And she knew that it could mean ruin for Paradise. If she didn't call them, they wouldn't leave their homes. If she didn't call, the night creatures would never sleep again. Her tear dropped, slicing through the air to land below her just at the oak tree's base. She watched the earth drink it up, saw the shoots of new life come from it. What would it be? Lavender, geranium, feverfew? She would never know.

The Sun grew brighter, but Phoenix felt only cold. Cold and urgency. All around her, the flora and fauna waited for her siren. They were awake now, just waiting for the call that would announce the day had begun. They twittered with need to venture, to eat, to drink.

Why hasn't she called us yet?

What's wrong with Phoenix?

Should we do something?

She's never failed us.

She heard their thoughts, their worry flushing throughout her own body.

Phoenix panted faster, the cold taking hold of more than just her heart. Her body began to shake. She closed her eyes. If she could just call out one last time, her final song, they'd know and know what to do.

The warm scent of cinnamon and clove wafted from her nest. She'd not remembered grabbing the spices on her flight the day before. *Some rituals never die*, she thought.

The forest's panic rose. The trees shuddered, bark creaking, in their desperate reach for control. The animals skittered in their homes, running round and round in tight, little circles of fear. The owls stayed in flight, back and forth above the canopy just waiting. The hoots thin and desperate. She could even feel the insects and worms. She'd vibrate out of her body soon if she didn't do something about their energy.

She looked to the Sun, and begged, "Please. Just once more. Then you can have me."

With that, she felt the white-hot cold turn to flame. She didn't have to look down to know what was happening. The spices burned around her, their incense clearing her lungs, preparing her. She stood then, stretched her wings once more, and trumpeted her final song—loud, long, proud—flames blending with her ruby and gold wings, the smoke of her cremation sending her melody echoing far beyond the reaches of Paradise.

And as the trees shook off the dew, the squirrels pittered and pattered, the owls settled in for their rest, all that was left of Phoenix was ash.

Paradise grieved. For three days, the owls slept. For three days, the trees shook. For three days, the squirrels pittered and pattered the forest floor.

Paradise wailed. And the flora and fauna suffered from the exhaustion.

And then…whoosh! A brief spark and flame erupted from Phoenix's nest. All stood still, waiting.

What was that? asked the trees, trepidation stopping them statue still.

Hide. Hide. Hide, worried the squirrels, nibbling their paws.

Be calm, whispered the owls, finally rustling from their sleep. *Just wait.* The owls had seen this before. They knew, as they always did, just what was coming.

And as the last rays of the Sun kissed Paradise, all heard a little cheep and peep from the nest. They saw fluff and feathers fuss and flutter as baby Phoenix rustled out from under the ashes. She hopped on the side of the nest, no bigger than the squirrels. She shook her wings, down and white in their purity—the gold and ruby would come in soon enough—ash cascading to the forest floor beneath her. And the earth swallowed it, replacing it with sprouts and pups and shoots of new lavender, geranium, feverfew, of oak, elm, ash, of sagebrush, willow bush, juniper, of it all. She shifted and shimmied in her nest, ash puffing up to the leaves of trees, new buds popping where it landed. Then, she settled and closed her eyes.

That small peep was all they needed. The trees stopped shaking. The squirrels curled up in their holes. And the owls took flight with the first rays of the Moon.

Tomorrow, Phoenix would wake Paradise and call the owls back to rest. But tonight, she would sleep her first sleep in this new life.

Mother Cardinal's Price
To my mom whose lessons forever inspire me

"But, Mother, wh-hy!?! I don't wanna leave the nest today." The little fledgling huffed in deep and then sighed so audibly it hung in the air. He stuck his pouty beak out. Mother Cardinal felt her heart tug a bit. She didn't want Little Bit to ever leave the nest, but she had a responsibility. They both did. So, she closed her eyes and counted to ten, slow, before answering.

"Son, it's important. It's our role, what we must do for this world, what we're meant to do." She hopped on the branch until she was close enough to envelop her son under her left wing. "And sometimes we have to sacrifice what we want for others. Otherwise, the world is chaos." Her fledgling stood stiff under her wing but didn't hop away. His little heart thumped—one, two, three, four, one, two, three, four, one, two, three, four, one two, three, four. She could almost hear the pace echo throughout her own hollow bones. His breaths came quick, too. She exhaled. How her soul reached for him, wanted to keep him there, too.

Mother shook her head and looked down at her son. "I know you don't want to go, Little Bit, but you must. I can't do it alone." She squeezed him in closer, patting her own feathers against his wing.

"Harumph. Fine." He ducked under her wing, not looking at her. "What am I to do?"

"Just follow me, young one." And with that she shimmied her body, flapped her wings, and pushed off the branch, her son following close behind. Immediately, the wind's current caught them, sending them in just the right direction. Mother Cardinal looked to her son, flying so strong, so in control, and shed a lone teardrop.

***

Mother Cardinal settled on the sycamore branch first, fluffing her tan and red wings and then folding feathers against her sides. Her little fledgling stumbled beside her, teetering and tottering as he landed. He mimicked his mother, only his own blood-red wings entangled before finding their place on his back. She smiled. *This he still needs time to practice,* she thought. Mother and son looked ahead of them to the human home before them, stone and unmoving, so different from their own nest of twigs and bark and grass braided and woven with love. On the porch, they saw a human male, swaying on the swing. The crick and creak of the wood as it swung, front to back, echoed to the birds. The man's slumped shoulders shook as he hugged himself.

"Mother, what's wrong with the human?" Little Bit asked. He tipped his head right, then left, a short peep slipping from his beak. Mother Cardinal clacked her beak as she watched her son watching the human.

"Well, Little Bit, he's sad, so very sad." Her eyes glistened before she blinked and refocused on her sweet one, seated next to her, soon to learn one of life's hardest lessons. Little Bit sucked in deep, exhaling a quick sigh. He clicked his beak back at her.

"Don't be frustrated, sweets," Mother began. "Just watch." She nodded her head toward the human man. He stopped swinging, leaned over, elbows on knees, head in hands. Wailing wafted around them. Her own eyes welled up. She sniffled, quiet and slow, as she felt the man's grief, understood his loss.

Little Bit brought his wings in front of his face, ducking his head. "Oh, that sound. It's breaking my heart." The little fledgling's own shoulders began to shake. She heard him sniffle and cough as drops plopped down on the branch in front of her. Her own heart seized. *Maybe he isn't ready? Maybe he needs more time?* She shook her head at her thoughts. She knew that came from her own desire to keep him, always, by her side. She pecked at his head, light and sweet, and cooed at him.

"Yes, dear one. That's the sound of loss, of grief, of the emptiness left when one we love no longer walks with us." She lifted her right wing to his, tugging lightly at it to uncover his face. She lifted his chin, forcing him to look at her. "Just as I would be if anything happened to you." She leaned over then and nuzzled his head, closing her eyes. He nuzzled back. Mother blinked until her worries cascaded down her tawny face, following the veins of her feathers, slipping onto her son's red, red wing and down to the branch they perched on. They mixed with the slight puddle of his tears, mother and son's empathy swirling together, melding. She watched and promised herself never to forget this moment.

"Can we help him, Mother?" Little Bit whispered. "I want to help."

Her heart pumped faster just then. She lifted her head, a sad, sweet smile spreading across her face. "Yes, my love. But it's too soon for the human. We'll check back next week and the weeks after until his pain is less. Then, I will teach you the most precious gift we cardinals give to others."

***

Four weeks later, mother and son perched on that very same branch, watching their human friend as they had every day since that first. Little Bit had led the way for the first time, sailing on the current, tipping right and left at just the right moments, landing smooth and delicate. Mother Cardinal had followed behind, slower than before, trying not to burst into her own wails. This time, the man sat on the porch swing, still sad, only his sadness slid down his face slowly, one at a time. No shoulder shake. No wailing. Just the emptiness of his grief.

"Mother, I don't understand. How can he still be so sad?" Little Bit settled his wings, folding one atop the other on his back. Mother felt her stomach flop, first with pride at his growth then with that deep, sinking feeling every mother gets before the nest is empty. Soon, she knew. Soon.

Mother Cardinal turned back to the man, felt his loss wrap around her own heart. He no longer emitted waves of desperation. Now, she felt only longing, only loneliness. She knew the time had come. Her own loss held hands with the man's in her heart. But she had a responsibility.

"Grief is the price we pay for love, dear one," she began, still focused on the human's emotions. "And love is the most important thing we all do." She looked to her son and let that seep in a minute before continuing. "But now, Little Bit, now is the time for you to help him. See, we cardinals have a special job in this world. The Universe deemed long ago, at the beginning of life, that we would be the ones to help humans through grief and back to love." She looked at her son then and saw his own eyes swelling with loss. *So he too feels it. That's good.* She cocked her head left and right and smiled down on her fledgling son, so close to leaving the nest altogether. *Soon,* she echoed in her mind. Her heart gripped, just for a second. She took a deep breath, and it pumped.

"How do I do that?" These five simple words from her dear one had been what she'd waited for all this time. Yet, she closed her eyes to quiet her grief.

"It's simple. All you do is fly to a place where you can land so that he sees you. And then sing, my darling." Little Bit turned his head, shoulders falling a bit. She hopped to him, again wrapping him in her wing, perhaps for the last time. "You see, dear one, cardinals are the eternal reminder of those they have lost to the afterworld. We bring them a moment of peace and memory of their dead. And for some, they believe we *are* their loved ones, reborn to come watch over them."

She watched as his eyes flickered, his brain working out what she'd just said. He perked his shoulders up, straight but soft. His eyes fluttered, open and shut. He looked to the human man, creaking back and forth, back and forth, then down to his own feet gripping the branch. She watched as he followed his legs, his body, outstretched his right wing first, then his left, each time following to the tips of his wings and back up, carefully looking. He folded them back behind him again. Then he looked to her, his crest perked.

"It's our red, isn't it? It's like blood and family and love." His words chirped out fast, almost as one. His mother felt his gaze deep in her heart. She closed her eyes, pride pumping through her.

"Yes, Little Bit. It's the color of your wings. Though I can serve as a symbol of their loved ones, it's your crimson that connects them."

The man hiccupped a cry as he swung. Little Bit turned back to him then.

"He needs a reminder, doesn't he, Mother?" She just nodded and patted his wings folded against his back. He looked at his mother, nodded back, and flew away, landing on the crape myrtle in front of the man, the magenta flowers shuffling as he settled. The rustle startled the man, but when he saw Little Bit's bright, lovely red, his hands covered his mouth, left atop right. And then Little Bit saw his smile creep out from behind his hands. Little Bit looked back to his mother, who nodded at him, so he hopped a little closer, reached his beak out, and peeped his youthful call, stuttering at first but then finding his rhythm.

When she heard the long song followed by four quick chirps, Mother Cardinal knew this would be her last time to see her sweet son. Little Bit would become the adult cardinal he was destined to be. And she would remember him always, his call, and when she'd hear it, she would know that he was helping another human. And she'd sing back.

Rayshell E. Clapper lives and loves in Martinez, CA, where she spends her time with words as a writer and a Professor of English at Diablo Valley College. She began her teaching career in 2002 and has found her dream job at DVC. She's deeply involved with the literary community of her campus bringing authors to read, hosting the biannual Literature Week, and planning mini-workshops for creative writers. She loves teaching about the power of words, helping students tap into that power, and spreading her enthusiasm for writing and reading.

At the tender age of four she wrote her first story about a duck and an elephant, which her mother still has. She was hooked and has written since then. She earned her Master of Arts from the University of Oklahoma concentrating in Creative Writing (theory and craft) and American Literature. She then earned a Master of Education from East Central University in English Education. In 2019, she completed her Master of Fine Arts from the Red Earth MFA program at Oklahoma City University. Her manuscript of short stories includes fables, fairy tales, fantasy, and mainstream literature. But truly, all her work has a little bit of mythology and the faerie, even that which is based in reality. She's been published in several virtual journals including *Dragon Poet Review, CyberSole, Sugar Mule, redOrbit,* and *Steam Register.* She's most honored to have Finishing Line Press publish her chapbook collection of fables.

Mythology and fairy tales are her passion. When not reading for her job, she spends most of her time in these worlds, reading classical myths and fairy tales as well as modern re-envisionings. These are her favorites.

Beyond words, she draws inspiration from spending her time outdoors: hiking, camping, gardening, and exploring. She grounds herself in Nature and the earth. She credits this to her Virgo sun. Nothing will calm her more than walking in nature or digging in the dirt. And her plants bring her such peace and joy.

She's blessed with two dogs—Leeli and Corsi—and one humongous cat—Big Ben. Together they provide each other much love and therapy. She's also blessed with a partner who loves her (and puts up with her fussiness) and provides support and space for her to grow.

The most important thing in the world to Rayshell is love. She loves deep and eternal. Her partner, her friends, her family, and her plants and pets inspire her to grow and be her best self to love and support them.

When not loving words, Nature, pets, or her people, Rayshell can be found learning something new. Everything is an opportunity, and she grabs onto those as often as she can.